Ten Little Monkeys
jumping on the bed

illustrated by
Tina Freeman

Child's Play (International) Ltd

Ashworth Rd, Bridgemead, Swindon, SN5 7YD UK

Swindon   Auburn ME   Sydney

© 2001 Child's Play (International) Ltd   Printed in Heshan, China

ISBN 978-0-85953-137-5   HH1509178X811171375

20

www.childs-play.com

Ten little monkeys
jumping on the bed,

One fell off
and bumped his head.

Mother called the doctor,

And the doctor said,
"No more monkeys
jumping on the bed!"

Nine little monkeys
jumping on the bed,

One fell off
and bumped her head.

Eight little monkeys
jumping on the bed,

One fell off
and bumped his head.

Mother called the doctor,

And the doctor said,
"No more monkeys
jumping on the bed!"

Seven little monkeys
jumping
on the bed,

One fell off
and bumped his head.

Mother called the doctor,

And the doctor said,
"No more monkeys
jumping on the bed!"

Six little monkeys
jumping on the bed,

One fell off
and bumped his head.

Mother called the doctor,

And the doctor said,
"No more monkeys
jumping on the bed!"

Five little monkeys
jumping on the bed,
One fell off
and bumped her head.

Mother called
the doctor,

And the doctor said,
"No more monkeys
jumping on the bed!"

Four little monkeys
jumping on the bed,
One fell off
and bumped her head.

Mother called
the doctor,

And the doctor said,
"No more monkeys
jumping on the bed!"

Three little monkeys
jumping on the bed,
One fell off
and bumped his head.

Mother called
the doctor,

And the doctor said,
"No more monkeys
jumping on the bed!"

Two little monkeys
jumping on the bed,
One fell off
and bumped his head.

Mother called
the doctor,

And the doctor said,
"No more monkeys
jumping on the bed!"

One little monkey
jumping on the bed,
She fell off
and bumped her head.

Mother called
the doctor,
And the doctor said,

"NO MORE MONKEYS
JUMPING ON THE BED!"